ROLLER COASTER LOVIN'

BY: HOWARD BOONE JR.

THIS BOOK IS A WORK OF CREATIVE EXPRESSION. SOME NAMES, SITUATIONS, AND IDENTIFYING DETAILS HAVE BEEN ALTERED OR IMAGINED TO PRESERVE PRIVACY.

EDITED BY: HOWARD BOONE JR. & JAMIE STEVENS

PUBLISHED IN THE UNITED STATES OF AMERICA

ISBN: 979-8-218-91875-0

FIRST EDITION

TABLE OF CONTENTS

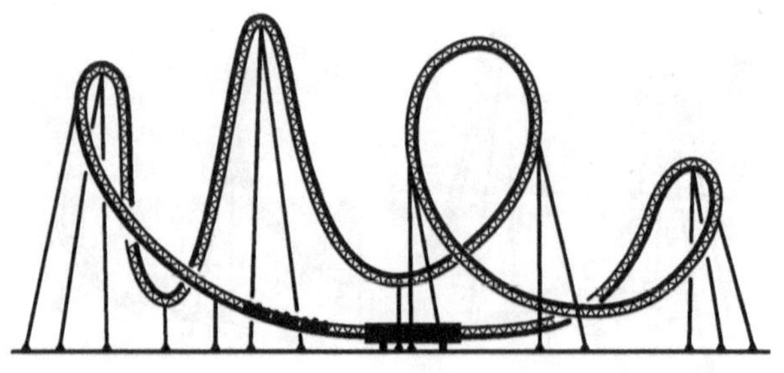

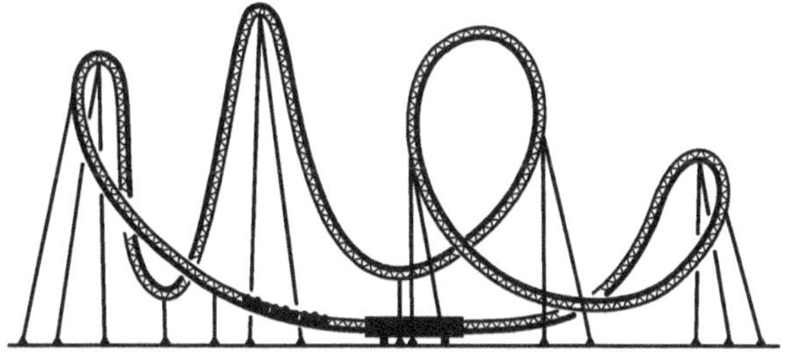

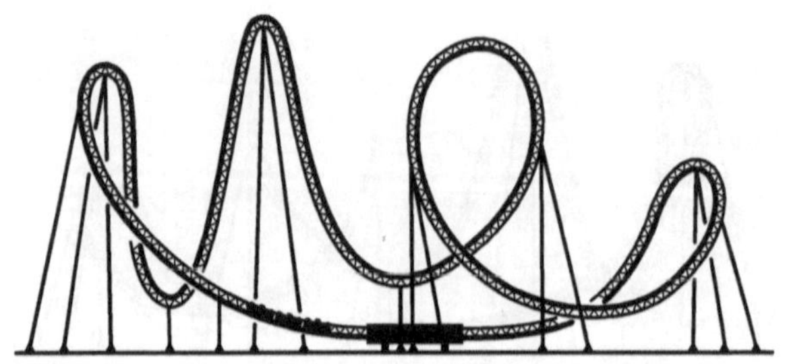

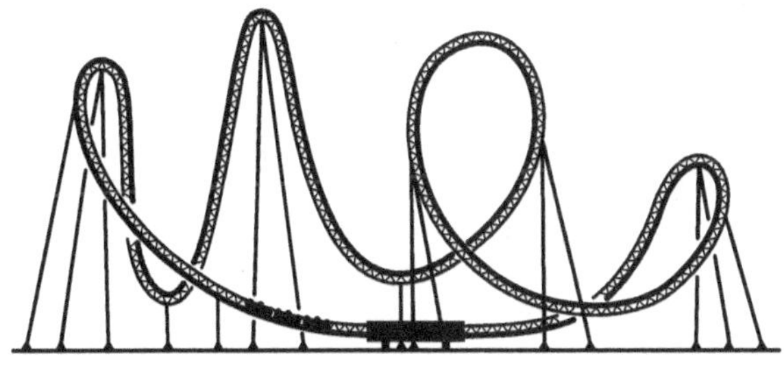

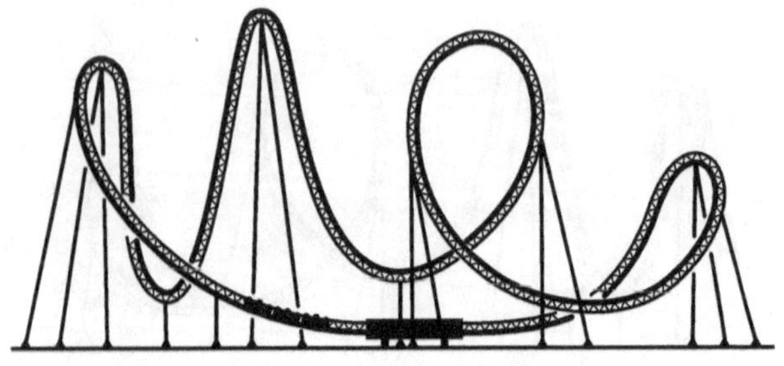

INTRODUCTION

Love can be a dangerous game.

Either endless and forever, or for personal gain.

Do my feelings match the things that I see?

Envisioning roses and not an inch of that flower brings peace.

Love is like a musical song.

It can sound like the 90s and still be objectively wrong.

Tears precipitate like rain.

Through these thunderous eyes I plan to incubate this beautiful pain.

Trusting in God that I may finally feel what I see.

Roses of peace and love, restoring all the grace within me.

WHERE'S YOUR SAFE SPACE?

Magical moments on a daily, or maybe I'm just crazy.
I can't deny these feelings yet my mind is kind of hazy.
The good outweighs the bad though the road is fairly shaky.
I'm on cloud nine but I need to land safely.

So let me just mention, while I have your attention.
The vibes you display is the reason I'm conflicted.
One minute we're good, then the mood is quickly shifted.
Communication is what usually can ease all the tension.

I understand your pain, I understand your past.
I want to help you heal so that our love never crash.
Don't worry about your flaws, I love you for you.
Growing old together is what I truly want to do.

ONE OF ONE

Love is not a crime, I just want you mine.
A flex without a sweat, I love the way you shine.
Independent woman, working hard nine to five.
Her heart is of a hustler, she's loyal to the grind.

No time for the games, never known for wasting time.
Chasing all her dreams, somewhat motivating mine.
Ambition is her aura, her odor by design.
Can't another one compare, she's made one of a kind.

LOVE NEVER ARRIVED

Tell me what are we waiting for?

Are you choosing me for the rest of your life?

Don't make our love this difficult.

Don't make me question if I'm the love of your life.

If I'm not the one just tell me.

I will wear this loss with pride.

Heartbreak has never been easy.

Why am I not that perfect guy?

HOLD IT STEADY

Music to my ears.
Rock me like a baby.
Laid up against your body.
Away from all temptation.
This is where I'm meant to be.
Cuddled up, just you and me.
Let's dive into forever.
Lifetime company.

THE TALES OF A NARCISSIST

The nerve of you to think.
You can shit and it not stink.
Afraid to own your wrongs.
When clearly there's missing links.

Splashing inside toxic puddles.
All our garments dripping wet.
Creating joy just for a moment.
Left soaked in more regret.

BAECATION

Trips and excursions.
Executed diversions.
Mimosas on the beach.
Tonight, cigars and bourbon.

A last-minute getaway.
Someway to take the pressure off.
Sick of being overworked.
Booking trips after every cough.

YOU GOT GAMES ON YOUR PHONE?

Chastising at a high rate.

Phone on vibrate.

Every single buzz, you assume there's a hot take.

I tell you what's the buzz.

The reason for the ring.

If you can't value my word, I short the claim I bring.

TETHERED RELATIONS

Simple guidance.

Raw connections.

Tight alliance.

Intensified affection.

BORROWED AMOUR

The mind can be swayed.
Desperate bites of the bait.
From words that are played.
Intentions to manipulate.

Eager to find love.
Obsessed with being accepted.
Harming hearts along the way.
Destroying passion and affection.

EASY, BREEZY, BEAUTIFUL, YOU

Beauty doesn't come from cosmetics.

Definitely not measured in aesthetics.

Beauty is overlooked in genetics.

But beauty should give the heart posture more credit.

BLINDED BY IGNORANCE

I gave you time after time.
That time just went to waste.
Time to look clear in the mirror.
See your impurities face-to-face.

Sheltered in avoidance.
Choosing the comfortability you know.
Instead of owning your mistakes.
Then wonder why people come and go.

LOVE ECHOES

You know how to tempt me.
I'm amazed at what you do.
The way you play it off so cool;
It's real.

The many ways you kiss me.
Activating my weakened knees.
Promises are never empty;
They come filled.

WHITECAPS

Cry me a river with never ending rapids.

The nature in this water is our unstrapped baggage.

Left to flow in peace until it's triggered.

Tranquil waters turned hostile from what's remembered.

CLINGY

Untouchable.

Yet, we feel so close.

If I was a superhuman loving you from miles away,

I'd teleport the most.

ATTRACTIVE LIABILITY

Every time you call,
I'm quickly reminded
The reasons why I fell back,
and never responded.
Your skin glowing bright,
was so awfully blinding.
Hiding all your toxic traits,
without trying.

THE KICKOFF

Call your girls on the phone, say no need for them to wait.
Let 'em know that you are safe and my home is where you'll stay.
Heating you up when it's cold with a pulsating warm embrace.
Cuddle season has arrived and we're now underway.

If you feel a stronghold, please be advised.
This magnetic pull attached to us can't simply be denied.
I'm all that you need, just tell me what you want supplied.
The things we desire both coincide.

SILVER FOX

Can you get it together?

Can you focus on me?

I'm running out of options, honestly.

I'd probably rather be single.

Totally care and stress free.

Even though growin' greys ain't a bad look for me.

HOME IS WHERE YOU ARE

Love me like you miss me.

Miss me like you care.

Genuine satisfaction.

Indescribably rare.

Wrap your arms around me.

Hold me 'til I'm warm.

Love me in the sunshine.

Build a bond through the storm.

HUNGER GAMES

Show me what it is,

I'll show you what it'll never be again.

Why stab me in the back,

near the spine that always bends.

Played my heart for the gold,

and my love for the win.

Violated my trust,

there's no way we can be friends.

MATCH MY REACH

Stretch your arms out a little bit further.
Show me how far they can extend.
I know I'm expected to lead from the front.
I just need your motivation on the backend.

Stretch your arms out a little bit further.
Show me the depth of your limits.
For richer, for poorer, in sickness and in health.
Can you love me the same without the winnings?

YOUR EYES LEFT FIRST

Wandering eyes speak volumes.
Maybe it's best that we stay friends.
Enjoy your other options.
Keep chasing that perfect ten.

I won't compete with a stranger.
Hands down I know I'm the better man.
Her eyes are curious about it all.
Right now I'm battling a fairytale.

LOVE IS EARNED

You fell into my arms so broken.
A handful attempts to piece you back.
In the past, many lies were spoken.
Something that you just can't quickly unpack.

Let me help you manage your damages.
Heal you from your soul down to your feet.
I know you are afraid of love vanishing.
A good man that can love all days of the week.

WRONG FLAVOR, RIGHT PERSON

This ain't for everybody,
when it comes to my love.
There might be somebody,
all they need is enough.

If you're looking for mediocre,
this ain't the place to find it.
No more wasted time,
nor endings without alignment.

HOLIDAY WONDERS

I refuse to be that guy,
who sabotaged your image.
I can be your sailor man,
that loves you like his spinach.

Trust what we established,
leave behind all the baggage.
If you decide that you gon' stay,
you won't regret you hadn't.

UNEVEN SCALE

Handling adversity;
Feel like it's got the worst of me.
This love ain't what it was supposed to be.
Both beautiful and ugly.

I'm right here where my heart desires.
Even when it's best to leave.
The battle between the back-and-forth.
It's clear I'm congested consciously.

MELANIN IN HARLEM

She's in love.

You can see it every time that she walks.

She's in love.

You can hear it every time that she talks.

She's in love.

It's the glow reflecting off of her face.

She's in love.

With a vibe that can't be replaced.

ESCAPING HER MIRAGE

I tried hard to make it perfect.
Thinkin' it was worth it.
I really just kept playin' myself.

To think it was for certain.
Knowin' I was hurtin'.
While you laid up with somebody else.

No longer will I be,
foolish and naïve.
Breakin' free from your lies I believed.

SOMEWHERE ON SOUTH BEACH

Balcony.

Sunset.

Baecation.

Good rest.

Beach strip.

Sundress.

Shades on.

Fit check.

TRAPPED IN ORBIT

My heart wants to flee for the things that she's done.
Her eyes want to cry for all the lies I've spun.

Somewhere in between the drama there's a King and a Queen.
Fed up with all the nonsense but scared to just leave.

This is a quick debrief of a relational hell.
Bonded by agony and can't unweave the spell.

SPEED BUMPS & TURBO FLUTTERS

Take it slow.

Calm it down.

Maintain control.

Tell me what you want from me.

I need those butterflies.

You know, that thing that brings me joy.

Don't just think I'm satisfied.

Give me so much more.

LIMITED HEARTS

Good people are hard to find.
Don't treat them like it's easy.
Good people get taken for granted.
They give an inch and a few get greedy.

Unconditional love is worth more than rings and labels.
Words smothered in trust without hands hid under tables.
Dangerously in love but still emotionally stable.
The most delicate parts of people should be gently cradled.

INTERLUDING THOUGHTS

-There is a high-level of responsibility in the way we carry ourselves in this world. Some people are living in the truth of others, that lack discipline and self-control.

-I thought we were both on the side of love where communication was endless. Bringing a better version of yourself in hopes for peace because of the things you have seen and experienced. Instead, you release a puerile nature when accountability is the main focus of conversation.

-Currently living in an era where remembering phone numbers has no significance anymore. At the same time, I find it ironic that as soon as I delete your number, I recognize the first six digits without reading the last four. This is a ten-digit combination linked to a person who no longer wanted me to love them.

SWEET FACED MENACE

If you were a fly on the wall at night.
You'd see the pain that you left on this side of the bed.
Breathtaking words that gave me life.
Believing every syllable within the lies you said.

I'll give you credit for some things thus far.
Like, pretending you were more than you are.
Faking a façade like you were created on Mars.
Created uniquely to leave emotional scars.

Gaslighting me to make me think I have found the one.
Slithering in my life with venomous trips around the sun.
Leaving your imprints while manufacturing distance.
No intent of commitment, just inconsistent existence.

UNMEASURED TREASURE

Treat my love like your intentions are to find gold.

Then see how serene it feels for my tenderness to unfold.

Treat my love like it was the best tale ever told.

Encounter warmth through happiness when the weather is cold.

ABANDONED BROWNSTONE

Graffiti on the wall like we stood under the beltway.
Layers stacked on layers, imperishable on the bricks laid.
Colorful stained memories of dismay.
The trauma from unanswered questions are hidden inside this place.

Sunlight beaming through what was once a rooftop.
Thin walls where you could hear a few pins drop.
Left for spectators to only be used as a backdrop.
Unknowing the unknown of the hardknocks.

PITY BE GONE

This parade will only consist of sunshine.

No small drops of rain can flood this home.

Happiness in every step that's before me.

The path we walk on is trailed by imperfect stones.

SAME FREQUENCY, DIFFERENT STATION

Why try and change me?

Am I not who I said I would be?

Am I not who I said I'd become?

Do I no longer possess the shining armor of a knight?

I was everything to you in the beginning.

Checking off all the boxes to your checklist.

I eventually became distasteful to your satisfaction.

Reconstructing your checklist to believe I'm nonexistent in your future.

FOREIGN LEVEE

I see you're timid.

Very much protective.

Putting several barriers all around your heart.

This could be different.

Only if you let me.

Show you a new approach to love.

FOR THE STREETS

Commitment to poor decisions.

One of many reasons I get offended.

Expectations for you were high.

That elevation quickly descended.

Bragging out loud that you found better.

Dealing publically with the same lessons.

I bet that season was a waste of your time.

I hope you kept the receipt for your ugly sweaters.

Sometimes you should keep quiet.

Relationships will humble you.

Portraying more of a hopeless romantic.

Relations you seem to stumble through.

HER BIGGEST FAN

Baby girl, don't be ashamed.
Evade the lack of self-confidence.
Your love handles are a national treasure.
Watch how they envy your opulence.

Excuse me if I stare while you dress.
Nothing new, but my eyes are impressed.
Forget all that is perfect and the social views of the flesh.
On your worst days I'll always see the best of the best.

CONCEALED BLEMISHES

She destroyed something good.
Put her scheming ways on notice.
She thought the grass was somewhat greener.
Until her shoe stepped over.

What's done is complete.
It's like missing early flights.
Tuck your vanity away.
It's overshadowing your light.

HONOR YOURSELF

I need more time to cherish love.
Lovin' on myself.
A season celebrating me.
Expectations of no one else.

When what's meant comes to be.
Now it's easier to breathe.
I'll replenish my empty cup.
So my heart is truly pleased.

OVERCROWDED INTIMACY

Everybody wants love without the effort to put the time in.
Too many people in your circle that feel the right to always chime in.
I knew there was a problem when I felt we were divided.
Taking advice from single friends, the folks you chose to side with.

The same hurt you once had is what you passed on to me.
There was trauma from your past and the healing won't complete.
Ignorant to think that there was a halfway we could meet.
Never again will I test my faith and make fatuous types of leaps.

THE QUIET STORM

I'm beyond energized with you.
Temperature ascending in this room.
Our time together creates a perfume.
Under the sheets we get stuck like glue.

Heaps of pleasure as I stretch out behind it.
Limited run space so don't you dare try to fight it.
You squirm away so I can pull you back in excitement.
Assessing my assertiveness for any further assignments.

LEFT IN THE GRAY

Why end on bad terms when we both know the truth?
I'm great for somebody, just not a great fit for you.
Those were your words when you spoke what you knew.
Now silence feels louder than what we've been through.

Still, through all your words I can't see your perspective.
Years of chasing closure but you're always deflective.
Reading old messages without being selective.
All that's comprehended is you being projective.

EMOTIONAL REFINEMENT

Growth is elevating your relationships.
Intimacy is rooted through friendship.
Even when you feel like the stars align.
The universe experienced is toured in separate trips.

Love wasn't created to be curated around you.
It was built for two individuals to be seasoned like stew.
Selflessly brewin' in the pot, sizzlin'.
Marinating in the spices cultivated from our differences.

MAP QUEST OF HEARTS

I just need a stress-free night so I can serenade a woman.
An ex will be an ex with random calls at any moment.
It's like a GPS is tracking me which forces her into losing it.
Calculating every turn like she knows just who I'm cruising with.

It won't be long until these women get annoyed.
The disturbance of a great time should be controlled and void.
But I let it happen anyway and both women felt toyed.
Deceitfulness will make anybody hate what they once enjoyed.

INTENTIONAL PLAYLIST

Songs that leave your heart feeling full and stuffed.

Reminds me of a person who I once truly loved.

Puts me in a state of someone feeling enough.

Connecting scuffed hearts that ain't scared to be buffed.

Seek love.

PRETTY FACE, DIRTY SHOES

I've been stabbed in the back and also lied to in the face.
If you listen to these words just know they come with bitter taste.
I will sit and tell the truth because my trust has been displaced.
Don't let the passion of my words have the message go to waste.

The fabricated lies you tell, undermine the real.
Even lying to your friends so they won't know the true ordeal.
They'll pick and choose your side, cause that's easily ideal.
Until what is done in the dark is exposed and revealed.

NON-VERBAL COMMUNICATION

A lot of times when we communicate,
we never have to speak.
The words are in our eyes,
the tightness of our cheeks.
Smiling through every second,
waiting for the perfect peak.
To honestly divulge our thoughts,
a developing mystique.

SAY SOMETHIN'

All I need is clarity.
Honesty been rarely.
Trying to work through it.
Communication been barely.

Pushing me away.
While my feelings go astray.
The doors are slowly closing.
Kinda hard for me to stay.

So if you really care,
like you say that you do.
The doors don't have to close,
and my heart can walk through.

MRS. ARRHYTHMIA

She got that super natural lovin',
that type of love that makes you weak.
An independent woman,
a freak under the sheets.

She got that supernatural lovin',
it will sweep you off your feet.
Somebody better call the doctor,
my heart just skipped a beat.

WHERE INTENTIONS MISALIGN

You applauded his mediocrity and then expected my perfection.
I exemplified excellence and you got more than you expected.
These doors don't open easily despite your indiscretions.
I guess I need to learn how to dumb down first impressions.

Doses of my love will have you overdosed with emotions.
Too much access of yourself can cause unwarranted commotion.
They can love you for the now, until the habits become a notion.
Words without meaning are only actions without motion.

BLESSING IN DISGUISE

The worst you could do is mismanage me.

During a season of growth with love harvesting.

Letting you go had to be my hardest thing.

Yet the promise God had was more promising.

BEBIENDO TEQUILA

Passion and sorrow.
Mixed with pecado.
Liquor at moonlight.
Unpleasant bravado.

Bring me tomorrow.
Two empty bottles.
Wake up at sunrise.
Throw up what I swallowed.

HEY LOVER, LOVER.... SWING

When you wake up next to me,
I'll be expecting a kiss.
This is how you start your day,
with a peck and a piss.
Your affection is like a full count;
hit and miss.
Before you leave and head to work,
come and take care of this.

FISHING ON DRY LAND

A man will be a man,
we'll do just what we do.
You ask and I respond,
but no belief in my truth.
If your past was that traumatic,
take time for you to heal.
Your hurt is ugly and it shows,
so careless with how I feel.

ASTRONAUT OF HEARTS

Let's indulge in something different,
get lost in the stars.
We can speculate the galaxies,
right where we are.
If you ever want a quick trip,
to Jupiter or Mars.
We'll spark up a natural herb,
enjoy a vacation from afar.

KEEP ON ROLLIN'

Bring me my keys baby.
Bring all your things when you come out too.
This chapter of my life is finished.
Locking all the doors that lead to you.

If you gonna weep baby, weep.
Shed all your tears before you leave this room.
A man like me will not be played.
But there are men who like the games you do.

She chose to be a mischievous lady.
She better be prepared for whatever comes next.
If you think I'm bluffin' just ask Shirley.
Also a few of my ex.

MY GEECHIE BABY

I make time to show you love, 'cause your comfort is what I seek.
Driving five hours for your heart, running off of no sleep.
Call me crazy and a fool for falling in too deep.
Oh well, I'm already here.

Presenting her the best without feeding her crumbs.
The approval of family granted with vertical thumbs.
Her smile keeps my heart pounding louder than drums.
Kisses that sparked flames until my lips became numb.

FLEAS & TICKS

Be careful who you lay with.

This gesture is very basic.

Save the heartbreak.

'Cause when it's broke you can't replace it.

You sneak, you cheat, you lie.

She thought she found her guy.

The way he navigates bullshit.

Surpass the natural eye.

ROLLER COASTER LOVIN'

This journey is about love.
This journey is about you.
This journey is about growth.
Watered by many truths.

This journey is about time.
This journey is about patience.
This journey is about transparency.
Nurtured by conversation.

This journey may come with twists.
This journey may come with turns.
This journey may come with bruises.
Varied by many terms.

INTERLUDING THOUGHTS II

-Unintentional people seek conditional relationships! A lot of what we think is genuine is only substantial until what attracted them to you is no longer desired or needed.

-Be unapologetic about guarding your heart! The energy doesn't have to come off rude nor nasty but understand that having a good heart attracts two types of people. Those who want to LOVE you for it, and those who want to USE you for it.

-Too much confrontation and not enough conversation. Better yet, people assume there will be confrontation, so they avoid conversation completely which ultimately leads to friction and separation.

-They say keep your friends close and your enemies closer. Right now, I'm not sure which side of the fence has your feet grounded.

TASTY IN BLACK

Receiving intel that you love that toxic shit.
Well, to your surprise I'm offering toxic d*ck.
I know it turns you on when I talk like this.
So gon' let me lick on that chocolate clit.

Every single touch is with a purpose.
Anything before me was basic and surface.
I set my standards high, damn near perfect.
So the intel I received in stanza one means nothing.

I can make you fall in love, no joke.
It'll only probably take me approximately four strokes.
Get my fingers wet and stick my hand down your throat.
Let you taste your juices from the cat 'til you choke.

PHEROMONES

Let me be obsessed with you.
Let me be a fan of you.
Keep my mind engaged.
Take the focus of your body.

All your curves are evident.
That alone is not exhilarant.
Vitalize my soul.
Use the fragrance of your heaven scent.

Anytime we depart, I thirst the hope of something more.
Your presence in the room is a sight that most ignore.
The protection of your elements sends critics in a roar.
Furthermore, you are a woman to adore.

SOUL SUCKING JEZEBEL

There's a brown skin lady.
She's been diggin' me for a minute.
This lady has only eyes for me.
I can tell 'cause body language shows plenty.

This brown skin lady.
She seems to know what she wants.
Her standards stand tall, but the roots are shallow.
All her wants are all the things that she won't.

I ain't gonna beg for it.
I ain't gonna forge my love.
I refuse to compromise with a leech.
It's probably safer if I let her walk away.

WRECKING BALL AT DAWN

Don't attempt to fall asleep before I safely make it home.
It might be late, but I expect for precious cargo to be thrown.
Unashamed to meet your pleasures since I know we both here grown.
The games I wanna play requires you with nothing on.

Don't let the time of the hour obstruct you from getting yours.
Your laced panties stitch with flowers will get lost down on the floor.
When I come home, I'm breaking off hinges.
Damaging private property starting with the very first door.

I HURT, YOU GHOSTED

The conversation doesn't have to be long.
It only takes a few minutes just to see whatchu on.
Don't expect me to leave a message at the sound of the tone.
Especially when you're looking directly right at your phone.

I tried to forgive, tried to extend you some grace.
Separated yourself and then communicated through space.
It's been months since we've seen each other face-to-face.
That's enough for me to rest my case.

So why did you lie, and where did you hide?
Waiting for many days, but months was passing us by.
Running from all your problems and you not even try?
The ghost of your presence was toughest goodbye.

VICTORY OVER VALIDATION

I see you miss what we had.
What you chased wasn't pleasurable.
Some people's hearts aren't pure.
Compared to mine, it's never measurable.

Now you feel the wrath.
What it means to not have access.
Availability on DND.
No need to slow forward progress.

It's crazy how you're back around.
When you once had called me weak.
Now rewarded of my worth.
You want to love me at my peak.

THE INSIDIOUS ALGORITHM

This topic right here makes me roar in laughter.
They say in life material things don't matter.
Boy, oh boy if my bank account was just a tad bit fatter.
I could cut out all the noise and a whole bunch of chatter.

At least that's what it seems, with all these media memes.
Spurious claims just to boost up the streams.
Damaged people damage people, only to leave you with dreams.
False narratives pushed to the extreme.

Nobody wants to fight through all the trials and tribulations.
They just want the good life, without cultivation.
Influencers with bothered souls can cause great manipulation.
What works for you is not for the world, and that's the frustration.

OVERQUALIFIED FOR HEARTBREAK

I'm not scared to commit.
Maybe trust just a bit.
We have our own expectations.
My heart won't grant limitations.

I'm not scared to admit,
I fall in love really quick.
If I say the three words,
I mean that shit.

However, I'm scared of rejection.
I second-guess myself and ask a million of questions.
In search of security but I'm left with neglection.
I don't need my ego stroked, at best some affection.

LOVE COSTS EVERYTHING

The love you confessed came with an agenda and plan.
Posing with a good heart and incautious where it lands.
Entitled to a love which only money could understand.
Grand totals on receipts is how you validate a man.

My heart still loves, just more alert with what comes near.
Grappling with these thoughts on how we wasted all these years.
If we never reconnect I highly doubt I'd shed a tear.
For the years we were together this was exactly what I feared.

Loving me for a price tag and not loving me for existing.
You loved you found a man that could afford things on your wish list.
For my love I would give it all, without the slightest of resistance.
A materialistic human can have you plummet in an instance.

ADJOIN ERROR

I said what I said but let's talk it out again.
I'd rather be your lover than considered a friend.
To act like I didn't miss you, that would all be pretend.
My reactions to your actions I can't begin to defend.

Trying to fight the urge, but my body was fidgety.
Sweating through my palms, I was feeling it mentally.
Triple texting her phone before the strong winds of lucidity.
Clutching on my ten toes to hold me down with stability.

Ahh damn, our passion once displayed in love has derailed.
Showing up unannounced, leaving hazardous trails.
That kitty-kat got dominion, now I'm hounding her tail.
Misaligned with my own essence, wrapped in an anomalous shell.

CRYPTIC LOVER

I don't mean to take your time.
Let me quickly invade your space.
There's something I need to say you.
These words can't be retraced.

I wrestled an eccentric experience.
Enhanced by your appearance.
When I spoke my words were garbled.
Phonetic tones weren't fully transmitted.

I hope you know that I love you when I fail to express it.
If my words become choppy, look in my eyes for expression.
The emotions are all there just without valid affection.
I'm a lovebird in pursuit of love, needing a healthy sense of direction.

BLUE'S CLUES

If you seek you'll find, things that play the mind.
Going through my phone, that's where I draw the line.

Don't become a mastermind, trying to piece together messages.
Attitude and arguments, two things that never settle shit.

If you seek you'll find, things that might trigger you.
Going through my phone, looking for things that might blow the roof.

Don't become impulsive, like I never kept you in the loop.
I was always honest, so don't act like you ain't know the truth.

I WAS THE PROBLEM

Temptation in my back pocket,
postponed until I need a favor.
At home I feel alone,
forsaken heart left on a hundred acres.

I went and found a safe space,
somewhere I felt someone relates.
Every excuse to leave the house,
so I can vent and get a taste.

This became so frequently,
'cause at home there was no chemistry.
Temptation was my enemy,
I battled infidelity.

AJNA CHAKRA

I want to talk about it, but I let some things just fade away.
Styled my room with all black drapes, to better contemplate.
In this state of mind please do not question how I meditate.
I close my eyes with every sigh, envisioning love in a better space.

Several missed calls and not one returned at all.
I am knee-deep in my thoughts, but standing high and walking tall.
A time to reflect so I can process all my flaws.
The hardest part for healing is when you start to have withdrawals.

This is a journey of a man seeking enlightenment and peace.
Awareness beyond logic and vision for the unseen.
Love can take you places that your mind won't allow to breach.
Only an opened third-eye gives you tons of wisdom without speech.

EXHAUSTED ARTIFICATS

If this love is not giving,
I'm done trying to give it.
Pack my bags and hit the road,
live life and start living.

Someday I'll try again,
but right now I'm not with it.
When things are done and final,
let it go and don't relive it.

So when this love stops giving,
I hate to admit it.
I am returning all of your things,
don't need an old exhibit.

WAR LETTERS

It's been months and I thought my mind had let you go.
Bouncing back from an all-time low.
In a world where I felt I had all control.
Still every thought of you gets me emotional.

If only you could observe your ways through my lens.
Visualize the love that you made end.
Signed breakups with inky pens.
Using ballpoints was a hurtful send-off.

GAMBLING ON THE FRONTLINES

I'm fighting for your love because I see the potential.
The heart can be fragile, so play with it gentle.
Don't make this complicated when it all can be simple.
Protective of my feelings 'cause my heart's presidential.

I'm coming in strong with the force like a train.
Open up your heart so you can show me your ways.
I can make a hellish day turn into beautiful pain.
I'm the type to love your imperfections and never complain.

Best friend, lover, somebody that you prayed for.
Love don't cost a thing,
but your smile could probably pay for it.
Tongue tied and paralyzed in the moments I should say more.
Lost for words, heavy at the feet nearing your front door.

TRENCHES OF LOVE

Drowning in confusion,
backstroking through the bullshit.
Dodging all these bullets,
but my heart still caught a full clip.

Bleeding through my words.
My heart, I can't seem to patch it up.
Speaking before I think.
My thoughts ain't moving fast enough.

My words begin to slur.
What I hear is not what's heard.
This conversation took a turn.
Tons of bags thrown on the curb.

PALE WILLOW

Moving on ain't easy, I just make the hurt look good.
Undetected troubles in a location I once stood.
If time could go back; I wish it really would.
Unhear all the words that I clearly misunderstood.

Saying that you love me with no meaning behind it.
Going through the motions, there's no way to deny it.
Guide me to your heart, not a quest to go find it.
Detached all your emotions and we quickly divided.

But now I know the truth, you were pickin' and choosin'.
Steady searchin' for a win but consistently losin'.
Your liberty to find better, I find horribly amusing.
This block ain't meant for spinning 'cause I'm done with recruiting.

THE WEIGHT OF YESTERDAY

Enemies change but love never dies.
When your heart is filled with passion all you can do is cry.
Some folks ain't stand a chance against the cutthroat of time.
In this life you gain your wings before you learn how to fly.

My heart gets colder on the chilly nights and rainy days.
Hopeless with the smudges from the hair grease on the windowpane.
Thinking about the good times, and why it couldn't stay the same.
People come and go like a migration in a season change.

INTERLUDING THOUGHTS III

-It's apparent that your heart wants love that your body won't let you explore. There's a disconnect between the words you express and the actions you display.

-Everyone loves different, but when you know better you do better. If your love ever came from an environment with degraded soil, your understanding of time and management is precious. Rushing the love that you desire doesn't disqualify you from the maintenance it requires, it makes you responsible.

-People are quick to acknowledge when someone no longer benefited them relationally, but never the accountability on how they mismanaged you mentally and emotionally. Their love required something transactional and all you requested was honesty that didn't come at the cost of your peace, and an understanding that didn't make loving you feel like a burden.

3AM IN CAROLINA

If my cup was spilled over, by someone you didn't know.
Could you help me clean it up, suppress the pain that overflowed?
Mishandled by a handful, that truly knew me most.
As the sun cycled through, my transgressors became ghosts.

Those you trusted to be in your corner, left you out to rot and dry.
Kept my trust tucked away, 'cause my heart was grieving lies.
"Call me if you need me", straight to voicemail the nights I tried.
Body full of exasperation, my joy and happiness had died.

1-800-LOVEDOC

Relationships are gentle,
know how to talk.
Be mindful of what you say,
and more careful with your thoughts.

Relationships are fragile,
have tough skin.
It's your obligation to stay grounded,
through the thick of the wind.

Relations aren't meant for the weak,
It's built on foundation.
A strong bond,
that can withstand vibrations.

JAMIE & FANCY

I will support your dreams when times get hard.
I will support your dreams with no regard.

I will support your dreams without the thought of tomorrow.
I will support your dreams in the days to follow.

I will support your dreams and become your number one fan.
I will support your dreams when you doubt that you can.

So let me support your dreams because I believe in you.
Your dreams are now my dreams and they despise me too.

BLURRED ARRANGEMENTS

Started out as study buddies,
then it ended with lovin'.
First it was casual touchin',
then it was intimate rubbin'.

It all was innocent,
just friends with benefits.
Intentions started to shift,
I pushed away a bit.

Boundaries were crossed,
without the thought of the cost.
Even though we both want more,
I'd prefer we not get lost.

TOTTEN'S LOVE STORY

First, I wasn't interested, but then she went to speak.
She graced me with her presence, with the pearliest white teeth.
Her style was of the essence, even though we sat oblique.
I complimented her all night, like my mouth had sprouted a leak.

She felt the high vibrations, so she asked could she switch seats.
Proceeded around the table with the curviest physique.
I tried to play it cool, but I smiled from cheek to cheek.
Double dates are not my thing, although I'm interested to see.

When I felt the vibe was mutual, it made my night complete.
I was anxious for a second, then that feeling had released.
I asked to take her home to seek how things could probably be.
She offered me another night, and quickly I agreed.

CAUTIONARY VULNERABILITY

I want to be transparent but I am somewhat afraid.
Scared that you will throw my flaws right back in my face.
I should voice how I feel 'cause this ain't a safe space.
Assuming if you knew it all, there won't be any grace.

I kept my guard up so I can avoid that hurt.
Became lackadaisical and let my heart fall in the dirt.
If this was love, why did it send so many alerts.
The type of signs we disregard to make nothing work.

HALIFAX CT. [SIDE A]

I am parked outside.
Let's go for a ride.
All we need is a word.

My tank is on E.
I'll fill up at pump three.
Take the risk of lovin' on me.

My windows are tinted.
Great for late night conversations.
All I want is your attention.

Don't fear makin' decisions.
Just put me in position.
Of course, only with your permission.

TIPPING TEAR BUCKET

They cried in this bucket,
until the bucket overflowed.
They cried in this bucket,
until the day that I came home.

They cried in this bucket,
with tears just for show.
They cried in this bucket,
for reasons I'll never know.

They cried and they cried in this bucket, till the bucket fell over.

BREAKFAST BY THE VINEYARD

Woke me up with smiles.
Breakfast by the pounds.
Laid it all out with some juice to wash it down.

The day was very special.
Or so I let myself believe.
Until alarms went off and I woke up from my dream.

How could this be?
Quick flashes like a glitch.
Somethin' Kodak moments can't get.

WORDS WITH FRIENDS

She was quick to blame me for the things that I say.
She said my words were projected in an insecure way.
This is the operation and playbook of the games people play.
Because she was the real reason why I felt pushed away.

I mean damn, why do I have to be insecure.
For speaking on the things that shouldn't have to be reassured?
On several occasions I expressed concerns, but bluntly ignored.
So I will speak my truth until I know where we stand is for sure.

ARTISTIC ROMANCE

Trying to paint the picture,
when nothing is ever perfect.
Loving you on purpose,
seeming so damn worth it.

But if it's never perfect,
can you help me paint the picture?
Drawing our perspectives,
paying very close attention.

To every little flaw.
To every little angle.
To every stroke on the canvas.
The trauma untangles.

LOONEY RABBIT

Why do you always start the day,
acting foolish.
When I address your manners,
you begin acting clueless.
Save the silly games,
for someone that is toothless.
Apologies are overused,
your words become useless.

INFATUATION

Everybody wants a taste of the streets.
Until they see a woman like you attached to a brotha like me.
Then they try to take a piece of your peace.
A piece of a man that is faithful, but bash the ones who cheat.

What we have can't nobody relate.
We both bring plenty to the table, including the plates.
Using us as a mental escape.
Duplicating in their mind what they see with irregular shapes.

LOVE-STRUCK FOOL

To never and forever.

Useless plucked feathers.

Hoping to find better and left with unsatisfied pleasures.

Put you up on a pedestal.

Something so intangible.

Made you feel entitled to a lust that wasn't marital.

So I put the blame on me.

I made myself believe.

That this immature feeling could be an everlasting thing.

VITAL SIGNS

Head is hurtin'.

Mind is racin'.

Stomach is turnin'.

I just can't take it.

Flooded emotions.

An offbeat flow.

Ups and downs.

Highs and lows.

SELF-SABOTAGE

I spoke too much,
love grinded on a clutch.
I spoke too soon,
then my words became a crutch.

In the process of becoming,
beautiful and stunning.
Love was the goal,
but looked for reasons to start running.

NATURE'S ROAR

We don't need the lights to prove I'm drowning.
Don't need backlit clocks to show the time.
When your legs start to shake, it's perfect timing.
I know exactly what's on your mind.

What we both need is entertainment.
Set your waters free tonight.
Navigating your body with amazement.
Scratch my back with your nails when it feels right.

LUMINESCENCE OVER WOLF CREEK

Under the stars is where I sit.
Crawled through my window for a second to vent.
Who I once was, was very confident.
Tonight, cognac relaxed through every sip.

Under the stars feel like therapy.
Rooftop views for better clarity.
Tonight I wish for more regularity.
So tomorrow ain't fueled by barbarity.

NOISY RENDEZOUS

I'm on my way over,
so we can pick up where we left.
Ready to cause some commotion,
touchin' in ways you won't ever forget.

Creating a passion,
leaving lovely fumes in the air.
Furniture thoughtlessly rearranged,
I still handled you with care.

UNCUFFED WINTER

Falling asleep anxious with an unsettled mind.
Hoping that you'd arrive with every peak through the blinds.
Wrong place, wrong person, and just a clock without time.
Folks use the word love, and don't know how it's defined.

This ain't easy when you feel all alone.
Cuddled by so many pillows, it feels like you're home.
Swiping through old memories when I look through my phone.
At night it gets chilly with no warmth to my bones.

HIBERNATING HEARTS

Isolated healing.

Inside the darkest of caves.

No way to catch any feelings.

Lost in the number of days.

Sounds of emptiness.

INTERLUDING THOUGHTS IV

-Mastering the art of becoming gentle. You owe it to yourself to walk with peace.

-The heart can lack judgment, so we pick and choose where we think love lives rather than where love made itself available and present.

-The benefit of walking away and letting things go last longer than the pain you will encounter trying to pour into the wrong people.

-Manage your relationships properly for the sake of your peace. Every person does not merit the same energy from you.

-Don't lose the best part of yourself trying to prove it to someone who doesn't believe in you.

THE BUS TERMINAL

I was waiting patiently.
My time had ended wastefully.
Roadmaps twisted into confusion.
Lead my full heart to function vacantly.

Sacrificed the smallest flaws.
In return it held the biggest pause.
I took a chance and waited.
Love lingered around for nothing at all.

HALIFAX CT. [SIDE B]

Meet me at the park at midnight.

I'll be waiting by the swings.

This is just a one time invite.

Testing what this love may bring.

When you walk down the driveway,

use the stars as your guide.

Make your way down to Peace Street,

a place where worlds collide.

NOT-SO HALLPASS

This was supposed to be a break,
temporary and not too long.
This was your idea,
now you suddenly moved on.

Finding out through the grapevine,
that your break was such a great time.
Allegations of a baby,
but somehow it ain't mine.

HEADED OVER THE HILLS

I thought you were there for me.
You said you would care for me.
I thought we would fall in love.
Live life ever happily.

I ran and told everybody.
Runnin' and skippin' blocks.
This ain't just anybody.
Gave 'em keys to unlock special locks.

STIMULATION WITHOUT THE STIMULANT

There was a chemistry physically,
no connection there mentally.
I thought I could call it love,
without elements that hit spiritually.
So let me just mention,
I exhausted my energy.
They say love can be blind,
but disregard liabilities.

SENTIMENTAL LOVER

Tell me I'm dreaming.

Explain the meaning.

I can't grasp why lifeless roses are in my hand.

I'm a fiend for more.

My ego is sore.

I can't give up on love even if my dreams do.

OUR NSTO'S

Natural laughter with a soothing tone.
Finds a good time when home alone.
A goofy woman like her wins.
She calms my nerves, I let her in.

Tall, handsome and intelligent.
Knows how to speak to me with confidence.
When he talks, I listen well.
I love this man and he can tell.

NOT WHAT BROKE ME

Dance into the sunlight.
Groove until the love comes back.
Open up your hips baby.
Release and let your past unpack.

Don't let trauma win.
Find your peace in love.
Growth should not be measured.
Let God be your judge.

MIDNIGHT MARAUDERS

Pullin' all nighters make me feel like I'm in high school.
You know I'm shy but that's the signs that show that I like you.
In a daze thinking 'bout some things that I might do.
Just know these kisses come with awkwardness and some bites too.

Love me like a 90s album.

OBSESSED WITH OPPORTUNITY

She wants to rush into things, only to be like the rest.
I want to take it slow and try to give her my best.
She wants to take cute pics, only to flex on her ex.
Claiming she's happy and moved on to the next.

Don't burn this bitch down trying to play both sides.
Check your ego at the door or take your ass back outside.
If this is gonna work I need all bullshit aside.
Just don't drag me along to keep your narrative alive.

CANDY SHOP

I hope you know I'm like sweet honey.

One taste will have you stuck on me for days.

If slow sensation is what you're craving.

Come get this sweet and sticky for a few hours of play.

DRAFT PICKS & BACK UPS

Red flags all around,
like love became a sport.
They competing for a spot,
somehow always come up short.

They complain and want to plea,
that the ball won't on the tee.
But if you're good when you swing,
you can't strike out after three.

BEYOND THE SURFACE

This is not about sex.
Let's make that clear.
I need a partner with substance.
Someone to pique my ear.

I want real conversations.
Articulate with delivery.
Speakin' with passion.
Permanent impressions on my memory.

CONTINUAL ELLIPSIS

I thought I moved on and overcame the validity.
Fell through the cracks and landed on vulnerability.
Went to send the text and it was filled with simplicity.
She replied, but it still did not fulfill the inner me.

Now I'm stuck on stupid and have nothing to gain.
I put my heart on display without hers beating the same.
Tried to reclaim a spark with some emotional flame.
She eventually stopped responding and it drove me insane.

KISS IT THROUGH THE PHONE

Random pics throughout the day expresses her mood.
She sends videos displaying some of the things that she can do.
Ready for me to clock out, ready for me to bring it home.
The evidence is proof that she no longer wants to be alone.

Now I'm finding ways to escape this workplace.
Distracted by her curves in the worst way.
Rush to the crib, without discussion we get straight to the foreplay.
Naked, like it's both of our birthdays.

UNATTAINABLE STANDARDS

After a certain amount of hours they say you become a pro.
I exceeded all of those numbers and I'm still your average Joe.
Somehow I'm thrown onto the curve with some cats she callin' bro.
Now her only use of words is a petty ass hello.

I did all the simple things that she thought won't realistic.
She wrote things down in her journal that kept her hopes optimistic.
As a woman she had craved for a man that's novelistic.
Yet the fairytale she fantasized required uncommon logistics.

RHYTHM & LOVE

Show me how you want to be loved;

I'll do it.

Dancing to the sound of your heart;

No music.

Speaking fire straight through to your soul;

So soothin'.

Body language from your caramel skin;

So fluent.

DROPPED CALL

I proposed a question,
looking to gain her perspective.
Her answer was respected,
though the energy was hectic.
Honesty was spoken,
her words just won't digestive.
At this point I'm listening,
but my ears aren't receptive.

THE UNSPOKEN FLAMES

This is not a common place where I would talk and be flirty.
Inside of church and during the middle of a service.
I tried to throw my charm on her but she knew I was nervous.
Something made me feel what she could possibly be yearning.

In her eyes I seen fire and through her words I heard desire.
Her tone screams that she's tired of all the cheaters and liars.
The things that I admired was her posie and her attire.
Her confidence is untouched despite the hurt she acquired.

DECEIVER

Everything was all good.

Vibes through the roof.

But the vibes change quick, when your love ain't the truth.

When the love is really lust and your heart can't keep up.

With your feelings on display.

These vibes you can't trust.

POV

It's the way you get to swangin' them hips.
When you look into my eyes I feel like a director, directin' a script.
It feels like static when I'm bitin' your lips.
If the homies know how I feel, they'll think that I'm whipped.

Between a man and a boy, you can tell that I'm rich.
My heart is filled with gold and I ain't scared to commit.
When you understand emotions and have true intent;
You can walk around unbothered when vibes feel like this.

LOVE BY SUBSTITUTION

I'm in love with someone else but somehow settled down with you.
My heart was in distress which made it easier to do.
Calling this true love when there's minimal proof.
Trauma bonding helped me tweak the truth.

My words that made you melt was when I thought about her.
I never truly healed so things with us have been a blur.
A blind man hides his lies and sees no fault for what's emerged.
Integrity is all I need heard.

HERD OF PAIN

I wear my heart on my sleeve,
it's constantly bruised.
In the middle of a stampede,
can't physically move.
Time don't heal scars,
they bury the wounds.
Suffering and the pain,
only God can approve.

FLINGS & TINGS

I'm just giving you full warning,
before sunrise.
I may be the one that causes heartbreak,
through soul ties.
I'm not here for forever,
just a good time.
Memories that quickly fade,
stored in the archives.

TIMED OUT

Revoking all access,
which you thought was allowed.
Like wanting yield from a harvest,
that you didn't even plow.

Don't prolong to tell your family,
I know they will be wowed.
Many viewed us as the blueprint,
just look at us now.

GOSSIP IS CHEAP, TRUST IS RICH

Many times I've talked to myself until my face turned blue.
In one ear and out the next, I guess this love is not for you.
Since you seem to have some doubts, first let's try to talk it through.
Don't gravitate to what they say unless you know for sure it's true.

I can't tell you how to feel but I can speak on what I know.
If they see us in distress they'll be waiting for a show.
They'll be waiting for a tweet and some type of crazy post.
But if we overcome the storm they can't understand the growth.

EMOTIONAL BACKROADS

It's midnight somewhere and I just need a reply.
Double textin' this chick, yet my phone is still dry.
Drivin' around thinkin' that you out here with some guy.
That's the only drunk explanation I can think of on the fly.

At this point I believe that I'm causing my own hurt.
This back-and-forth has made me walk through cruddy old dirt.
If love had many miles I'd probably sweat out 'bout five shirts.
Time to let my heart hit the road; I'm tired of being burnt.

OWN IT

She gets dressed without any makeup,
unbothered by her flaws.
Leaves the house close to how she wakes up,
no problem at all.

Confidence is what she brings,
it's hard to unsee it.
Curve game so strong,
she makes a man feel mistreated.

CHOSEN OVER, REMEMBERED STILL

She was supposed to be the one, I let her slip away.
Slipped right through my arms within a short amount of days.
I had bragged to my friends, how this girl was such a ten.
Now her heart is back on the market to be fluttered by these men.

To whomever is the man, competing with what I bring.
Just know that when she's with you, she'll still wish we were a thing.
I would test her love again, but she never doubles back.
Although for me she said she would, but has concerns for what I lack.

THE LURE

Talk real slow so I can fully comprehend.
Black love is magic, but these tricks ain't here for kids.

Vibrations from your body language ringing in my ear.
Tickling my soul, I swear you'll love it here.

Warming up the room without penetration.
Only simple touch and transparent conversation.

HEARTBREAK, ADHESION, & HEALING

Roses are red, and they say violets are blue.
After meeting you I learned that wasn't true.
Broke me into pieces in the year '22.
Picked up what I could and tried to fix it back with glue.

The war in my soul wasn't won by the weakly.
Mending a shattered heart ain't ever done cheaply.
This burden I had calloused wasn't lifted so freely.
In all the wretchedness I faced, my harmony returned completely.

So from this moment I will smile, and let God guide the miles.
The road may come with faults, but worriless of the trials.
No longer will I break, into microscopic pieces.
The learned lessons of distress, and the profoundness that it teaches.

HELD BY INTENT

I want to give you compliments as you walk through the crib.
Lay you on the couch while I take off your heels.
Make this routine like we’re practicing drills.
Taking every fantasy of yours and making them real.

Tell me about your day, let me know what's been going on.
Random affirmations to confirm we're still going strong.
Speak it to existence cause there's power upon the tongue.
If loving you is right, I fear the cost of being wrong.

PANTHERESS

I need a woman that is solid, when the sky is not blue.
Ready for the world of a man, when I say "I do".
Making way through the rapids, in a rocky canoe.
Unbreakable through it all, like steel toe boots.

I need a woman that is fearless, with a bold identity.
Walking in confidence, dressed down in serenity.
Ain't afraid to be alone, but ensures continuity.
Drawn together, by an undeniable affinity.

TALLADEGA HEARTS

This is what I had explained to you.

Don't waste my time, I have things to do.

Is you ready or not?, then drop the proof.

If love is a speedway, ride the truth.

Buckle up.

FOREVER BEGINS HERE

I will end this on a bended knee.
Complete all the things that were left incomplete.
A true King will have love presented at his feet.
The throne where he now sits is where his Queen gives him peace.

Finding hope in fragile pieces of myself as a scavenger.
Insecurities don't exist with someone of your caliber.
I will love you from the start, until the end of the calendar.
Measurements of love, trusting God as our balancer.

www.ingramcontent.com/pod-product-compliance
Lightning Source LLC
LaVergne TN
LVHW090611110826
845146LV00001B/344

* 9 7 9 8 2 1 8 9 1 8 7 5 0 *